Fruity Tunes

And the Adventures of Rotten Apple

Written and Illustrated by Jeanie Shaw

Also by Jeanie Shaw:
Jacob's Journey
My Morning Cup
Understanding Goose

Printed in the United States of America

ISBN: 978-1477609040

www.jeaniesjourneys.com

To Emma Kristen, Caleb Stephen, Alexandra Jean,
Micah Samuel, Emery Ann and Grace Melissa.
You are my sunshine!

From the author

This little story came to "fruition" several years ago as an interactive song and dance show for young children. It was created to teach young audiences about qualities that God desires—and to show them that good can overcome bad.

Fruity Tunes and her fruity friends have made a lasting impression on hundreds of children over the past few years. For this reason I want to pass this story on to my grand-children and their friends. My prayer is that many children can learn and enjoy the valuable lessons from Fruity Tunes and her fruity friends as they hear from them throughout the pages of this book.

There are several times throughout the book where you will have the opportunity to sing along to familiar tunes. So, grown-ups and kids—set your voices and imaginations free as you sing the songs. Also, since children tend to learn scriptures very quickly, many will be able to memorize the Bible verses used, such as two of Fruity Tunes' favorite scriptures:

> But the fruit of the Spirit is love, joy, peace, patience, kindness, goodness, faith-fulness, [23] gentleness and self-control. Against such things there is no law.
>
> Galatians 5:22-23

> Don't let evil get the best of you; get the best of evil by doing good.
>
> Romans 12:21 (MSG)

Fruity Tunes was a very happy grandmother. Every day she watered the fruit trees in her orchard. She loved to see the fruit grow. She also loved to sing while she worked. That's why her friends called her Fruity Tunes.

One fine, sunny morning while she was outside watering her orchard she heard some giggling.

Fruity Tunes looked around and under a tree she noticed a basket. She saw some funny looking grass and some beady eyes peering out from behind the basket. She wondered what could be hiding behind the basket, so she skipped over to see what she could find.

Behind the basket were some brightly colored objects. She saw red, yellow, orange and green things jumping up and down. Looking more closely she could see brightly colored fruit!

All of a sudden a bright yellow lemon jumped out from behind the basket.

"Hi," said the lemon, introducing himself. "My name is Loving Lemon. I love to give hugs, and I love to let you know that you are important to me.

"Do you like to give hugs? I do!"

Loving Lemon gave Fruity Tunes a big, giant hug.

He then began to sing, and Fruity Tunes joined in.
(Their song is to the tune of *London Bridge Is Falling Down*.)

"Loving Lemon loves to hug, loves to give, loves to share.
Loving Lemon loves you so. He's so loving."

While Fruity Tunes was singing with her new yellow, fruity friend a terrible, horrible thing happened.

A very mean and surly fruit fell from a nearby tree. This fruit looked much like an apple that had been rotting on a tree. In fact it was an apple—a stinky rotten apple!

Rotten Apple crept over to Loving Lemon and sang him a very mean song.

(All of Rotten Apple's songs are to the tune of *Three Blind Mice*.)

"I don't like you. You smell bad.
I don't like you. I hope you're sad.
I think you look funny and mean and fat.
You remind me of an ugly old rat.
I don't like you."

"You need to go away Rotten Apple," demanded Fruity. "You are not nice."

Fruity Tunes went to comfort Loving Lemon, who had begun to cry. But Rotten Apple would not move. Loving Lemon felt very sad.

Fruity Tunes had an idea. She called her friend, Tippety Teapot, who came running over to help her. "Tippety," Fruity exclaimed, "Rotten Apple is trying to steal away all of Lemon's love. We must help Loving Lemon!"

"I know what to do," answered Tippety. "Fruity, can you take my handle and help me pour out a song onto Rotten Apple? We will sing him a song and read him a Bible verse. Maybe that will help him!"

"Of course," said Fruity Tunes. "I'd love to help."

So Fruity Tunes helped Tippety Teapot tip over and they began to sing.

(All of Tippety Teapot's songs are to the tune of *I'm a Little Teapot*.)

"God is full of peace and joy and love,
So I will pray to my Father above
When I'm out of smiles and want to pout,
God says, 'Turn to me and I'll pour love out.'"

Next, Tippety Teapot pulled out her Bible and read a verse to Rotten Apple.

She read, "Dear friends, let us love one another, for love comes from God..." (1 John 4:7)

All of a sudden Rotten Apple slithered away.

"Hurray, hurray!!" Fruity Tunes, Loving Lemon and Tippety Teapot shouted. "We sure did make ol' Rotten Apple run away."

Next, Smiley Strawberry jumped up. Wearing a big smile, he ran over to join Loving Lemon. They gave each other big hugs.

"I'm so, so happy!!!" Smiley exclaimed. "I like to smile and to make others happy. I don't like to be sad...or grumpy. I like to be happy. When I'm happy, it makes me want to smile. Can I see how big you can smile?"

Meanwhile, behind the basket Patient Peach raised her hand. "Can I come out now?" she asked.

Fruity Tunes told Patient Peach that she would need to wait a few more minutes, as Smiley Strawberry was still talking and it was not yet her turn.

"Ok," she said. "I will wait my turn. I will be patient."

Then Fruity Tunes saw something scary in the distance.
"Oh, no!! Could it be? Do you see Rotten Apple again?" she asked Tippety.

Rotten Apple interrupted the fruits with his very mean and bad song.

"Do not smile. Just be sad.
Kick your feet. Be real mad.
I want you to be grumpy and mean and bad.
And disobey your mom and dad.
And do not smile."

Smiley Strawberry frowned and shouted, "Stop, Rotten Apple! This is a terrible song!! You are saying very wrong things! We want to be happy and to obey our parents. You are trying to steal our happiness. Go away!"

Fruity Tunes hurried to find a Bible verse to read to Rotten Apple. She read, "A cheerful heart is good medicine," from Proverbs 17:22.

Rotten Apple sure did need some of that medicine. The Bible verse was good medicine for Rotten Apple, but he would not take the medicine. He ran away.

"Whew, that was close," said Smiley Strawberry. "Now I can smile again."

Smiley Strawberry got his beautiful smile back.

As Fruity Tunes sang her favorite reggae song, "Don't Worry, Be Happy," another fruit appeared. This fruit had big green hair that Fruity Tunes had first seen behind the basket. This fruit was singing and dancing as she swayed over to Fruity Tunes and the other fruits. Fruity and the fruits could not help but join in.

Meanwhile, the green-haired girl spoke up. "Hi, Fruity Tunes and fruity friends. My name is Peaceful Pineapple. I am feeling so peaceful. I know sometimes I can worry... but then I remember how much God loves me and that fills me with peace.
Would you sing this peaceful song with me?"
(They sing to the tune of
Itsy Bitsy Spider.)

"The hurried, worried inchworm could not go very fast.
He felt sad that he always came in last.
He opened up the Bible; it taught him patient ways
And the hurried, worried inchworm had many peaceful days."

Suddenly this nice, peaceful song was interrupted. With another burst of meanness Rotten Apple stormed out!

"STOP the singing and dancing!" Then, in his angry voice he continued and sang his mean song.

"You be hurried—
Worried and scared.
You're on your own.
No one cares.
So cry and whine and be out of control.
Don't sing or pray or come out of your hole.
You be scared."

"Oh No!!" exclaimed Fruity Tunes as she realized Rotten Apple was now trying to take away Pineapple's peace. But Fruity Tunes, Loving Lemon, Smiley Strawberry and Tippety Teapot all knew what to do.

They decided to sing their special song to Rotten Apple and then read him a Bible verse. The fruits helped Tippety Teapot tip over as they sang. Tippety read a verse to Rotten Apple from Philippians 4:7:

"And the peace of God, which transcends all understanding, will guard your hearts and your minds in Christ Jesus."

Rotten Apple did not want to hear the Bible verse and again....he slithered away.

"Whew! That was a close one. Thank you for helping me stay peaceful, my fruity friends. Rotten Apple needs to stay away from us," said Peaceful Pineapple.

Fruity Tunes looked around and noticed Peach standing behind the tree, waiting patiently to join the other fruits. Fruity called to Peach.

"I'm sorry to keep you waiting Patient Peach. We want you to come join us."

She said to the other fruits, "Let's invite Patient Peach over to join us. On the count of three, let's shout, 'Come join us, Patient Peach!'"

"1-2-3, Come join us, Patient Peach!" called Fruity Tunes. "Now let's call for her in Spanish," she added.

Together, the fruits called out, "Uno, dos, tres!"

Patient Peach ran over to the group and asked, "Is it my turn yet?" She continued, "When everybody is interrupting and taking toys from others I will wait my turn. I feel so much better when I am patient. When I'm impatient, and get in a hurry...I get a pit in my stomach!"

This made Fruity Tunes laugh.

But just as soon as Patient Peach joined the other fruits the mean ol' Rotten Apple came calling again.

"Oh no!" cried Fruity Tunes and the fruits. "Now he is going to try to take away Peach's patience!"

Sure enough, Rotten Apple started chasing Patient Peach. He sang a very bad song to her.

"Give that to me.
I can't wait.
I want it now—
before it's too late.
I'll yell at you and interrupt while you talk.
I'll cut line and run over you when you walk.
Give that to me."

This time, they were all quick to act. They grabbed Tippety Teapot's handle, helped her tip over and then sang together.

"God is full of peace and joy and love,
So I will pray to my Father above.
When I'm out of patience and want to shout
God says, 'Turn to me and I'll pour patience out.'"

They opened the Bible and read to Rotten Apple. They read, "Be completely humble and gentle; be patient, bearing with one another in love." (Philippians 4:2)

Again, Rotten Apple ran away. They were happy that he ran away, but wondered if he would come back again.

He was behaving like such a bad, unhappy apple. What could they do to keep him away? They decided to pray about this. They prayed and then they had an idea.

Fruity Tunes called the whole gang together and asked, "What if together we pour out God's love, joy, peace, and patience onto Rotten Apple? What do you think might happen? Let's try it."

All the fruits agreed to try this plan. Gathering their courage, they called out, "Come on out wherever you are, Rotten Apple!"

Rotten Apple was very surprised and confused that they called for him...but came toward them with his less mean but confused expression.

Tippety Teapot began to sing as the fruits gathered in a circle around Rotten Apple. Fruity Tunes held Tippety's handle while they all sang to Rotten Apple.

"God is full of peace and joy and love
So I will pray to my Father above
When I'm out of smiles and want to pout.
God says, 'Turn to me and I'll pour love (joy) (peace) (patience) out.'"

As they sang to Rotten Apple, something amazing began to happen. The corners of Rotten Apple's mouth started to turn upward and he began to smile!

"Could this really be happening?!" the fruits wondered.

The fruits began jumping up and down with joy. The singing, praying and Bible verses they had poured out onto Rotten Apple changed him from the inside of his core! He was no longer rotten.

"From now on," the fruits explained, "we will call you Sweet Apple!"

"You were once mean and rotten, but you let God's love, joy, peace and patience change you," the fruits explained to Rotten Apple. "You learned the meaning of being God's fruits – just like the Bible teaches in Galations 5:22:

"But the fruit of the Spirit is love, joy, peace, patience, kindness, goodness, faithfulness, gentleness and self-control."

The fruits all gathered for a group hug, so happy that Sweet Apple was now their very special friend.

Made in the USA
Middletown, DE
08 February 2025

70883392R00018